Street Criers

OF THE

Marketplace

[1]

"FINE CHINA ORANGES.
PLAYBILLS!"

[8]

[7]

[2]

(A)

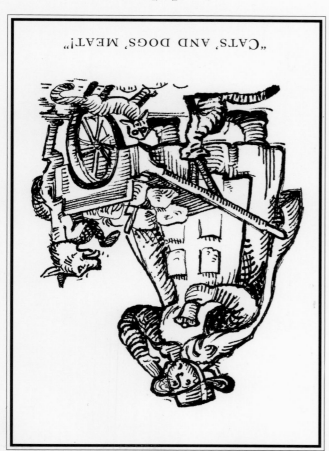

"CATS' AND DOGS' MEAT!"

"TOY LAMBS TO SELL."

Dream Peddler

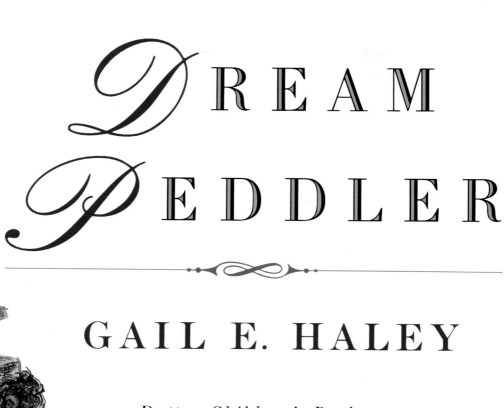

DREAM PEDDLER

GAIL E. HALEY

Dutton Children's Books

N E W   Y O R K

Library of Congress Cataloging-in-Publication Data
Haley, Gail E.   Dream peddler/by Gail E. Haley.—1st ed.   p.   cm.   Summary: A poor book peddler journeys
to London Bridge to find the answer to his dream.   ISBN 0-525-45153-6   [1. Peddlers and peddling—Fiction.
2. Dreams—Fiction. 3. England—Fiction.] I. Title.   PZ7.H1383Dr 1993 [E]—dc20 92-42074 CIP AC
Published in the United States 1993 by Dutton Children's Books, a division of Penguin Books USA Inc.
375 Hudson Street, New York, New York 10014   Designed by Adrian Leichter   Printed in Hong Kong
FIRST EDITION   10 9 8 7 6 5 4 3 2 1

"JOHN CHAPMAN, YOU MUST BE CRAZY!" JEERED AMADEUS the mountebank. "Your pack is so heavy you can hardly climb the hill without collapsing. Why do you carry so many books and newspapers? I've made more money in one day selling medicine than you can make in a whole week!"

"It's not money I'm seeking—and I carry more than books. In my pack are words, wisdom, ideas, and dreams," John answered.

"Words!" scoffed Amadeus. "What value are they? Look around you. Signs with pictures are enough to get simple folk through the day! What else do they need?"

John Chapman straightened his shoulders. His back hurt and his bones were weary. What Amadeus said was true. But how could John explain to other peddlers that he carried something that could not be bought at any price? He whistled for his dog, Caxton, and went on his solitary way, while the mountebank headed in the opposite direction, with silver coins jingling in his pockets.

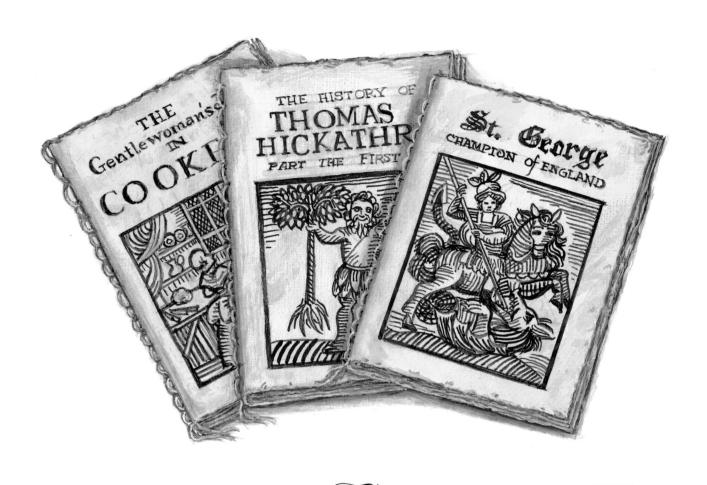

John Chapman was a seller of books. Wherever he went, villagers clustered around to buy the precious papers he sold for pennies.

Farmers waited for their almanacs and the news of prices their crops might bring. Housewives bought cookery books and useful guides on managing the household.

Dreamers asked for tales about adventure on the high seas or in faraway lands. Those in love chose garlands of poetry. Musicians wanted to learn the latest ballads and songs for dancing.

For children, there were primers for teaching the alphabet, sums, history, and geography, and sheets of singing games and rhymes. But the greatest treasures of all were the books of stories and fairy tales, which set the children's imaginations soaring.

Yet for all his hard work, John Chapman had only pennies in his pockets when he returned home at the end of his journeys.

His wife, Lydia, had to do extra baking to help the family survive. His children were more ragged than any others in the village. But they could read by the time they were old enough to go to school.

When the family gathered around the hearth, John read them stories that carried them far beyond the simple walls of their cottage. Their dreams were as rich as those of any royal children.

One night, after a hard week on the road, John Chapman had a dream.

He was on the highway without his pack, and Caxton was by his side. A booming voice came from the sky.

> "*If you will go*
> *to London Bridge,*
> *you will be told news*
> *to bring great joy*
> *to those you love.*"

In the distance, John could see London Bridge and the river Thames gleaming in the light of the full moon.

Then he woke, and that same moon was shining through his bedroom window. He could not go back to sleep, but lay thinking of what he had dreamed.

When morning came, John told the dream to Lydia and his children. "I must go to London Bridge. I feel it in my heart," he said.

"Nonsense. There is a hole in the roof, John," said his wife. "If you don't repair it, our upstairs floor will be ruined." So all that day they gathered straw, and John rethatched the roof.

That night, the strange dream came to John for the second time. In the morning, he was even more eager to be off.

But again, Lydia would not hear of it. "Oh, no, John. This is the very day when the vegetable garden must be planted. It says so in the *Goodwife's Calendar* that you yourself bought me."

John sighed and turned to his duties. He borrowed a horse and plowed the soil. They all worked together to break the sods and rake the earth smooth. By nightfall, rows of vegetable seeds were sleeping snugly in the garden.

That night, John Chapman's dream came for the third time. Lydia heard him murmuring in his sleep and knew she no longer could hold him back. She got up and packed food for him to take on the journey.

News of John's strange dream had spread around the village, and people gathered to watch him set off for London Bridge.

Simon the baker muttered, "It will take him six days to walk that far. He'd be better off helping me grind flour to pay off his bills."

Dame Purselip shook her head. "Those poor ragged children!
And poor Lydia. John is off on one more foolish trip."

But there were some who stopped and wished him well. They
were glad that he was willing to follow his dreams.

Days passed as the two travelers made their way toward London.
John's food did not last long, but Caxton managed to catch a rabbit
here and there. John earned food doing odd jobs along the way.

At night, they slept by the road, or in the ruins of deserted
buildings or walls, and wondered what adventure awaited them.
By day, they trudged on.

At last they reached the busy thoroughfares of London. The din was so loud that John had to cover his ears.

Carts and carriages rumbled along. The wail of a bagpipe accompanied the dancing of a pair of puppets. Street vendors and tradesmen cried their wares. And then the military tattoo of a passing regiment of soldiers drowned out all else.

Caxton got lost among the legs of strangers and took shelter under Tiddy Doll's gingerbread stand.

When at last John found his dog, they ran down a side street to escape the crush and confusion. Looking for a quiet place to catch their breath, they ducked into a nearby shop.

When John looked about him, his mouth fell open in amazement and delight. They had stumbled into a bookstore. It smelled of printer's ink and leather bindings. The shelves almost glowed with the rare colors of marbled papers and gilt letters on the ample spines of books.

John wandered from shelf to shelf, staring at the wonders he saw. He stroked the cover of a volume of *Aesop's Fables* and dreamed of taking it home to his children.

But when the store owner caught sight of John's tattered clothes and dusty dog, he pointed to the door and said, "No dogs are allowed here, sir." John set off once more, his spirits lifted by the sight of the beautiful books.

On London Bridge the road was crowded with wagons, carriages, and litters. In the windows of the shops that lined the bridge, John saw more goods for sale than he'd seen at all the country fairs he had visited. Pedestrians and vendors pushed along the narrow footpaths, and some tradesmen cried their wares in the streets or from their doorways.

At night, fellow travelers camped in the open plazas on the bridge. John read them stories, and they shared their meager food.

For three days John wandered up and down the bridge. He was feeling very foolish and discouraged. Even Caxton was getting snappy.

From the balcony above his shop, Morris the tobacco merchant watched this strange man. Finally, Morris hailed him as he walked by the shop front.

"My good fellow," said Morris, "I've been watching you walking back and forth, neither buying nor selling. Pray tell me why you are here."

"I'm afraid I'm on a fool's errand," said John. "You see, for three nights in a row I had a dream that told me to come to London Bridge to hear joyful news. I walked for six days to get here. I'm hungry and footsore, and I've heard nothing but the din of the city."

The tobacconist laughed heartily. "You poor foolish man," he exclaimed. "You spent six days getting here, three days walking about, and now you must travel back home for six days. That's more than a fortnight wasted! And it looks as though you could ill-afford such folly.

"I too had a dream for three nights in a row," he continued. "I dreamed that I was to go to a village called Swaffham and find the house of a man named John Chapman. The voice in *my* dream told me to dig under the apple tree in Chapman's back garden, and there I would find a box of Roman gold. Imagine that!" He laughed again. "I would never follow a silly dream. I am twelve days richer because I stayed here, minding my shop. Go home immediately and mend your foolish ways."

John followed the tobacconist's advice and headed home quickly. This time it was he who was laughing, for he had heard the good news he had come for!

When John finally returned to the town of Swaffham, he called to Lydia and the children, "Waste no time! Come out and help me dig!" So the family came out and helped him dig under the apple tree. They dug rocks, crockery, and tree stumps. Caxton dug a bone. Finally, just before dark, they struck an old metal box. John pulled it from the ground and broke the rusty lock. When they opened it, the gleam of the gold inside was brighter than the fading sunlight.

From that night on John Chapman was a rich man. He lost no
time in rebuilding his house and buying pretty things for Lydia
and the children, who'd had so little for so long.

With his family taken care of, he purchased the print shop where
he had bought many of the books he used to carry and read. There
John pursued his special love of words and letters, and he became
a maker of books as well as a seller. He labored long and hard,
bringing books to the people and teaching all to read.

The citizens of Swaffham were very grateful to John for all that he was doing for them. So that no one would forget the man who followed his dreams, they had statues of the peddler and his dog carved in the front pews of the church that John had rebuilt for the town. And the statues are still there to this day.

This story is derived from a folktale called "The Peddler of Swaffham," which had its origin in fifteenth-century England, although variants on the theme also exist in many other cultures. The version presented in this book is set in eighteenth-century England. During this time, English artists such as Hogarth, Gainsborough, and Sir Joshua Reynolds captured a culture in transition. Village life was giving way to the beginning of the industrial age, with small technical improvements occurring throughout the century. In the printing industry, which relates to this story, advances in technology accelerated growth in the number of newspapers and periodicals, which in turn came to lessen the importance of the oral tradition, ballad singing, and the newscaster bellmen, just as today's visual technology now challenges print.

During the latter part of the 1700s, when John Chapman lived, true books with hard covers and bindings were owned mainly by people of wealth. Poor people, who might own a Bible as their only book, read chapbooks, which were thin, pamphlet-like books. The *chap* syllable in the words *chapbook* and *chapman* derived from the word *cheap;* thus, chapbooks were cheap books. Chapmen were itinerant peddlers who sold cheap items such as trinkets, jewelry, and medicines, which they carried in cases. They also sold chapbooks, and printed sheets of paper, some of which could be cut up and sewn into little books.

HOW TO MAKE A CHAPBOOK

You can make your own chapbook by photocopying the endpapers from this book on two separate 8½-by-11-inch sheets of paper. Then follow the directions below.

1. Fold each page in half along line A, with pictures facing out.
2. Place the folded sheets on top of each other so *Street Criers of the Marketplace* is on top and to the right.
3. Fold in half along line B, making sure *Street Criers of the Marketplace* appears on top.
4. Staple or stitch on the fold along line B.

"CHERRIES RIPE!"

[6]

"TROOP EVERYONE."

[3]

[5]

[4]

"BAKING PEARS AND QUINCES!"

"BUY A FINE SINGING BIRD."